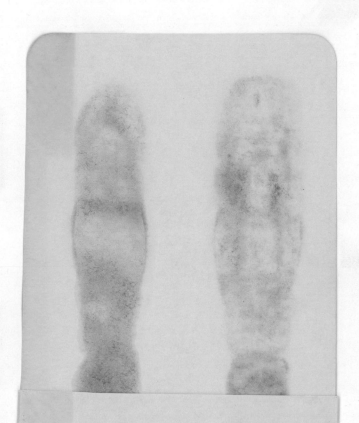

San Mateo Public Library
San Mateo, CA   94402
"Questions Answered"

21

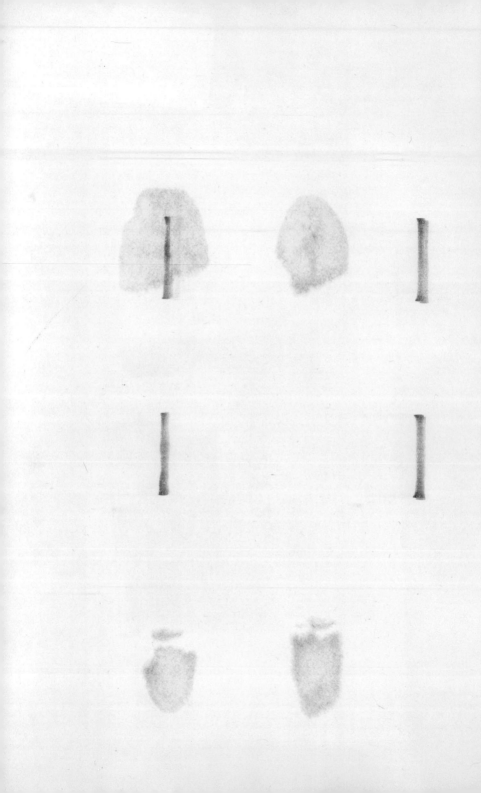

The Forces of Plenty

The Forces of Plenty

ELLEN BRYANT VOIGT

W · W · NORTON & COMPANY · NEW YORK · LONDON

Public Library San Mateo, CA

811
Voigt

Copyright © 1983 by Ellen Bryant Voigt

All rights reserved.
Published simultaneously in Canada by George J. McLeod Limited, Toronto.
Printed in the United States of America.
First Edition

The text of this book is composed in VIP Garamond, with display type set in Garamond lite.
Composition and manufacturing by Vail-Ballou Press Inc. Book design by Antonia Krass.

Library of Congress Cataloging in Publication Data
Voigt, Ellen Bryant, 1943–
   The forces of plenty.
   I. Title.
PS3572.034F6 1983   811'.54   82–14198

ISBN 0-393-01730-3

ISBN 0-393-30107-9 (pbk.)

W. W. Norton & Company, Inc., 500 Fifth Avenue, New York, N.Y. 10110
W. W. Norton & Company Ltd., 37 Great Russell Street, London WC1B 3NU

1 2 3 4 5 6 7 8 9 0

In memory of my parents

Lloyd G. Bryant
Zue Y. Bryant

Acknowledgment is due to the periodicals in which these poems first appeared:

Antaeus: "Letter from Vermont," "Blue Ridge," "Sweet Everlasting"
The Atlantic Monthly: "Daughter," "Pastoral"
Back Door: "Epithalamium," "The Happiness Poems," "Rescue"
The Georgia Review: "A Fugue," "January"
The Missouri Review: "Alba," "Liebesgedicht"
The Nation: "The Diviner," "For My Husband," "Jug Brook," "The Apology"
The New Republic: "For My Mother"
The New Yorker: "The Bat," "Talking The Fire Out," "The Spire"
The Ohio Review: "The Medium," "Year's End"
Ploughshares: "A Marriage Poem," "Eurydice," "The Gymnast," "Exile," "The Couple," "The Spring"
Poetry: "Quarrel," "Why She Says No"

The three sections of "For My Father" were published as separate poems by *Antaeus* (under the title, "Turning From A Loss"), *Poetry,* and *Ploughshares,* respectively.

It should also be noted that the first two lines of Section 3 in "A Fugue" are taken from Sir Thomas Browne.

I would like to acknowledge the generous support of the John Simon Guggenheim Foundation and the National Endowment for the Arts, whose help made possible the completion of this book. I also want to thank Louise Glück for her acute and articulate criticism of these poems.

EBV

CONTENTS

9

III

I

THE SPIRE

In the Bavarian steeple, on the hour,
two figures emerge from their scalloped house
carrying sledges that they clap, in turn,
against the surface of the bell. By legend
they are summer and winter, youth and age,
as though the forces of plenty and of loss
played equally on the human soul, extracted
easily the same low bronze note spreading
upward from the encumbrance of the village,
past alluvial fields to the pocked highland
where cattle shift their massive heads
at this dissonance, this faint redundant
pressure in the ears, in the air.

From the village, the mountain seems
a single stone, a single blank completion.
Seeing the summit pierce the abstract heavens,
we reconstruct the valley on the mountain—
a shepherd propped against his crook, birds
enthralled on a branch, the branch feathering
the edge of the canvas—transposing
such forms as can extend the flawed earth
and embody us, intact, unaltering, among
the soft surprising trees of childhood,
mimosa, honey locust and willow.

Wood in the midst of woods, the village
houses are allied in a formal shape
beside a stream, the streets concluding

at the monument. Again the ravishing moment
of the bell: the townspeople, curious
or accustomed, stop to count the strokes,
odd or even—the confectioner counting out
the lavendar candies for his customer,
the butcher, the greengrocer, the surgeon
and the constable—as the housewife
stands on the stoop, shaking her mop,
and sees the dust briefly veil the air,
an algebra of swirling particles.

A FUGUE

for Tom Moore, M.D.

1.

The body, a resonant bowl:
the irreducible gist of wood,
that memorized the turns
of increase and relinquishing:
the held silence
where formal music will be quarried
by the cry of the strings,
the cry of the mind,
under the rosined bow.

2.

The deaf listen
with compensatory hands,
touching the instrument.
Musicians also
listen, and speak, with their hands.

Such elemental implements.
The eye trains on a grid of ink,
and the fingers quicken,
habitual, learnéd,
to recover the arterial melody.

3.

The long habit of living
indisposes us to dying.
In this measured space,
a drastic weeping.

———

Music depends
on its own diminishing.
Like the remembered dead,
roused from silence
and duplicated, the song heard
is sound leaving the ear.

———

Medicine too is a temporal art.
Each day, children
are rendered into your keeping.
And so you take up your instruments
to make whole, to make live,
what others made.

4.

Pure science:
the cello in your lap;
the firm misleading bodies
of your own children
in your brother's room.
His illness is adult, and lethal.
You place the bow
and Beethoven turns again
from the stern physician
to annotate the page:
cantabile—
          meaning
not birdsong, windsong,
wind in the flue, bell, branch,
but the human voice,
distinct and perishable.

And you play for him.

JUG BROOK

Beyond the stone wall,
the deer should be emerging from their yard.
Lank, exhausted, they scrape at the ground
where roots and bulbs will send forth
new definitions. The creek swells in its ditch;
the field puts on a green glove.
Deep in the woods, the dead ripen,
and the lesser creatures turn to their commission.

Why grieve for the lost deer,
for the fish that clutter the brook,
the kingdoms of midge that cloud its surface,
the flocks of birds that come to feed.
The earth does not grieve.
It rushes toward the season of waste—

On the porch the weather shifts,
the cat dispatches
another expendable animal from the field.
Soon she will go inside to cull her litter,
addressing each with a diagnostic tongue.
Have I learned nothing? God,
into whose deep pocket our cries are swept,
it is you I look for
in the slate face of the water.

THE MEDIUM

My father struck me when I first told
what I had witnessed;
my mother plucked her beaded chain.
But no matter how I scrubbed my left hand,
the lines, like trenches, emptied into the palm.

Sixty years with these companions
who rise from exile
to pour their diminishing cupfuls into me.
Sometimes, it's only a breath swollen with fog.
Or a column of light on the stairs, by the cupboard,
displacing the air and its busy dustmotes.
But when I hear their pitiful signals of grief . . . .

———

The white field has risen over the fenceline.
I sit for hours by the window,
like any old woman.

On the west side of the house,
a drift flutters gracefully against the clapboards,
like the dress she wore to greet her lover
the night his knife dazzled into her body.

This is the Crown of Winter,
the last storm that can raise the level of snow.
Soon the sun will begin its hot subtraction.

———

A small square moon:
the neighbor's light in the distance.
Imagine,
her husband hunched over supper,
a child nested in her lap.
How could I have a life?
I was their tether,
the incompleted dead, the stubborn ones,

who will not forestall my own soul's slow erasure.
After my bones are put on their shelf
there will come the usual solstice,
not pain but the absence of pain,
terrible, unwarranted.
And then the second death:

a stranger will sleep in this bed without dreams;
will wrap himself against the evening's chill;
will credit the wind with my whispers;
will straighten the portrait again and again
without revelation;
hearing nothing, believing nothing.

THE GYMNAST

I have beaten the blank mat, but the name
that tolls from the wide throat of the crowd
is *Nadia, Nadia.*
Magic is not earned and is not fair.
After repeated labor against
the body's meat and strict bone, still
with each leap or press or stretch or somersault,
my flesh in its new attitude
mourns like a lover for the ground. And Nadia
balances on the dust beside the beam,
she takes the shapes of a leaf in slow wind.

Others climb after that mark;
I will settle
for the long hours of practice at her side,
my error reconciled in her correction—
mother and sister, midwife, teacher,
I am earth, earth, from which her body leapt into the air.

PASTORAL

Crouched in the yard,
he brings his dirty hands up to his mouth.
No, No, I say. *Yuck. Hurt.*

These are sounds he will recognize.
I say them when he takes an orange
with its hidden seeds and allergenic juice.
No. Yuck. Bad orange. Or reaming
from his mouth a wad of bread,
a lump of odorous cheese.
The fire will hurt.
The stick will break and stab you
in the heart. The reckless wheel,
the cool suggestive music of the pond.

Overhead, summer spreads its blue scarf;
a light wind bends the hollyhocks;
birds, trees—
everything the way I might have dreamed it,
he stands in the grass,
weighing a handful of berries,
a handful of stones.

THE SPRING

Beneath the fabric of leaves,
sycamore, beech, black oak,
in the slow residual movement
of the pool;
        in the current
braiding over the wedged branch,
and pouring from the ledge,
urgent, lyric,
        the source
marshalls every motion
to the geometric plunder of rock—
arranging a socket of water,
a cold estate
where the muscle wound
in the deep remission of light
waits
    for the white enamel dipper,
the last release, the rush,
the blunt completion

WHY SHE SAYS NO

Two friends at the close of summer.
On the path, the birds quicken.
While he talks,
he strokes her arm in one direction
as if it had a nap of feathers.
How handsomely the heart's valves
lie open for the bloodrush.
How her body also begins to open.
At the edge of the woods, they pass
goldenrod and lupin, the tall thin weeds
supple as a whale's teeth
conducting the avid fish to the interior.

She is not the mouth, whatever you think
and even though she craves
this closeness, its rich transfusion.
Desire is the mouth, the manipulating heart,
the wing. Above her,
the branches of the pines, their quilled expanse
blanketing the subtler vegetation.

THE DIVINER

The danger surfaced in the fontanel.
I held your head on my arm,
whispering lullabyes into your sweet hot neck;
by the second week that was forbidden.
Then you swam alone
on your white sheet. Robed, masked,
I put my face as close as I could get it
to see what the sickness pulsed and signaled.

———

When I was little,
my father used to light a Lucky
and blow warm smoke, like a secret,
into my sore ear. I was amazed
it never escaped through the other ear,
nor any orifice Mother peered into—
to be housing the breath of my father!

———

Now you are growing and closing
everywhere against me.
The melded hemispheres of bone
have sealed my small window
as I pace the dry ground with my wand,
trying to hold the stick without bias,
trying to learn what the surface will not tell,
until the green wood plunges, nearly twists
from my grip: there's water here—
but how much? and how deep?

ALBA

My daughter calls me into light to see
the world has altered while she slept.
Like my mother's voice that pulled me
from the clarifying dark, her voice
will not relent, a bell at my ear
rehearsing gladly for her own child
in whom my long thirst for sleep
will reappear.
                      Hush. Hush.
My work there is not finished.
Before morning overwhelms the house,
I must ford the tall grasses—
Then the circle of birches,
the stranger's face not yet in full shadow.

II

FOR MY HUSBAND

Is it a dream,
the way we huddle over the board,
our fingers touching on the slick button?
The Ouija stammers under so much doubt,
finally reaches L, then O,
pauses under its lettered heaven,
and as it veers toward *loss* and the long past
that lodges with us, you press toward *love,*
and the disk stalls
                            outside
a cry is loosed from the bay,
but you are looking for two swans
on a glass lake, a decade of roses—
oh my lonely, my precious loaf,
can't we say outloud the parent word,
longing,
            whose sad head
looms over any choice you make?

A MARRIAGE POEM

I.

Morning: the caged baby
sustains his fragile sleep.
The house is a husk against weather.
Nothing stirs—inside, outside.
With the leaves fallen,
the tree makes a web on the window
and through it the world
lacks color or texture,
like stones in the pasture
seen from this distance.

This is what is done with pain:
ice on the wound,
the isolating tourniquet—
as though to check an open vein
where the self pumps out of the self
would stop the second movement of the heart,
diastolic, inclusive:
to love is to siphon loss into that chamber.

2.

What does it mean when a woman says,
"my husband,"
if she sits all day in the tub;
if she worries her life like a dog a rat;
if her husband seems familiar but abstract,
a bandaged hand she's forgotten how to use.

They've reached the middle years.
Spared grief, they are given dread
as they tend the frail on either side of them.
Even their marriage is another child,
grown rude and querulous
since death practiced on them and withdrew.

He asks of her only a little lie,
a pale copy drawn from the inked stone
where they loll beside the unicorn,
great lovers then, two strangers
joined by appetite:
                              it frightens her,
to live by memory's poor diminished light.
She wants something crisp and permanent,
like coral—a crown, a trellis,
an iron shawl across the bed
where they are laced together,
the moon bleaching the house,
their bodies abandoned—

3.

In last week's mail,
still spread on the kitchen table,
the list of endangered species.
How plain the animals are,
quaint, domestic,
but the names lift from the page:
Woundfin. Whooping Crane. Squawfish.
Black-footed Ferret. California Least Tern.

Dearest, the beast of Loch Ness, that shy,
broad-backed, two-headed creature,
may be a pair of whales or manatee,
male and female,
driven from their deep mud nest,
who cling to each other,
circling the surface of the lake.

EXILE

The widow refuses sleep, for sleep pretends
that it can bring him back.
In this way,
the will is set against the appetite.
Even the empty hand moves to the mouth.
Apart from you,
I turn a corner in the city and find,
for a moment, the old climate,
the little blue flower everywhere.

BLUE RIDGE

Up there on the mountain road, the fireworks
blistered and subsided, for once at eye level:
spatter of light like water flicked from the fingers;
the brief emergent pattern; and after the afterimage bled
from the night sky, a delayed and muffled thud
that must have seemed enormous down below,
the sound concomitant with the arranged
threat of fire above the bleachers.
I stood as tall and straight as possible,
trying to compensate, trying not to lean in my friend's
direction. Beside me, correcting height, he slouched
his shoulders, knees locked, one leg stuck out
to form a defensive angle with the other.
Thus we were most approximate
and most removed.
                    In the long pauses
between explosions, he'd signal conversation
by nodding vaguely toward the ragged pines.
I said my children would have loved the show.
He said we were watching youth at a great distance,
and I thought how the young
are truly boring, unvaried as they are
by the deep scar of doubt, the constant afterimage
of regret—no major tension in their bodies, no tender
hesitation, they don't yet know
that this is so much work, scraping
from the self its multiple desires; don't yet know
fatigue with self, the hunger for obliteration
that wakes us in the night at the dead hour
and fuels good sex.

Of course I didn't say it.
I realized he watched the fireworks
with the cool attention he had turned on women
dancing in the bar, a blunt uninvested gaze
calibrating every moving part, thighs,
breasts, the muscles of abandon.
I had wanted that gaze on me.
And as the evening dwindled to its nub,
its puddle of tallow, appetite without object,
as the men peeled off to seek
the least encumbered consolation
and the women grew expansive with regard—
how have I managed so long to stand among the paired
bodies, the raw pulsing music driving
loneliness into the air like scent,
and not be seized by longing,
not give anything to be summoned
into the larger soul two souls can make?
Watching the fireworks with my friend,
so little ease between us,
I see that I have armed myself;
fire changes everything it touches.

Perhaps he has foreseen this impediment.
Perhaps when he holds himself within himself,
a sheathed angular figure at my shoulder,
he means to be protective less of him
than me, keeping his complicating rage
inside his body. And what would it solve
if he took one hand from his pocket,
risking touch, risking invitation—

if he took my hand it would not alter
this explicit sadness.
                        The evening stalls,
the fireworks grow boring at this remove.
The traffic prowling the highway at our backs,
the couples, the families scuffling on the bank
must think us strangers to each other. Or,
more likely, with the celebrated fireworks thrusting
their brilliant repeating designs above the ridge,
we simply blur into the foreground,
like the fireflies dragging among the trees
their separate, discontinuous lanterns.

THE COUPLE

"Like a boy," she said,
and opened her robe to show him
the plate of bone and its center flower
of black thread.
                    Only flesh, he thought,
the breast cut loose from its net of skin.
And if she could not dote on him,
he'd answer her bell in the bedroom
where she is lodged among the pillows,
her spread hair weightless,

but now he knows how heavy her head is,
how it rolls on her shoulder
when he pulls her off the floor,
how, as they stumble toward the bed,
old woman, old man,
he hears two threading voices—
the one stammering in his chest,
and the one who calls him in the thickening air.

EURYDICE

It bears no correlation
to the living world. It is
as if a malice toward all things
malleable, mutable,
had seized the universe
and emptied its spherical alleys.

How could you think it,
that I would choose to stay, or break
under the journey back? Like a dog
I had followed your unraveling
skein of sound—
                Orpheus,
                        standing
between me and iridescent earth,
you turned to verify the hell
I was thrown to, and got
what you needed for your songs.
They do not penetrate the grave,
I cannot hear them, I cannot know
how much you mourn.
                    But I mourn:
against my will
I forgive you over and over,
transfixed by your face
emerging like a moon across your shoulder,
your shocked mouth calling "Wife, wife"
as you let me go.

EPITHALAMIUM

for Keith

The river,
the white boat,
the moon like new money:

This is the union of air and water.

My husband moves easily
among the cluster of friends.
You stand at the rail to watch
the new couple,

until the two of them
leave the dream,
it having become a parable of longing.

I go over the side and down the rope ladder
into the muskrat house.
The walls are lined with mute, oriental faces.

I must be there to give instruction,
coming as I do
from my strong marriage,

but it is you who goes straightway
to the large book.

I'm sure it is you—
the characteristic raised knuckle,
the frame hunched with its own weight.

Earth shaping us on all sides,
I put my face against the cool mud wall:
this is our element.

———

Look, Keith:

on the shore
my husband builds me a fire.
The light pools on the sand.
It is this fire, his fire,
that weds us over and over.

Sal gives Elaine his open hand
and we stand in a circle
like four walls, each
of another color,

our shadows cast out
behind us into evening,
as, at the center,
the fire burns recklessly
to give us its definition.

QUARREL

Since morning they have been quarreling—
the sun pouring its implacable white bath
over the birches, each one undressing
slyly, from the top down—and they hammer
at each other with their knives, nailfiles,
graters of complaint as the day unwinds,
the plush clouds lowering a gray matte
for the red barn. Lunch, the soup
like batting in their mouths, last week,
last year, they're moving on to always
and never, their shrill pitiful children
crowd around but they see the top of this
particular mountain, its glacial headwall,
the pitch is terrific all through dinner,
and they are committed, the sun long gone,
the two of them back to back in the blank
constricting bed, like marbles on aluminum—
O this fierce love
that needs to reproduce in one another
wounds inflicted by the world.

YEAR'S END

The fingers lie in the lap,
separate, lonely, as in the field
the separate blades of grass
shrivel or grow tall.

We sat together in the little room,
the walls blotched with steam,
holding the baby as if the two of us
could breathe for him and were not helpless.
Upstairs, his sister turned in her sleep
as the phone rang—

to have wakened to a child's cry,
gagged and desperate,
and then repeat that terror when the call
split the quiet house and centered
its dire message:
                           a child was dead
and his mother so wrung by grief
she stared and stared
at the moon on its black stalk,
the road glistening like wire.
Rubbing the window clear of steam
as a child rubs sleep from its eyes,
and looking past the fence to where
he had plunged the sled up and down the hill,
we could still see the holes his feet made,
a staggered row of graves
extracting darkness from the snow.

When morning brought the new year in,
the fever broke, and fresh snow
bandaged the tracks on the hill.
For a long time we stayed in the room,
listening to him breathe,
like refugees who listen to the sea,
unable to fully rejoice, or fully grieve.

LIEBESGEDICHT

I love you as my other self, as the other
self of the tree is not the pale tree
in the flat hand of the river, but the earth
that holds, is held by, the root of the tree.
This is how the earth loves the river,
and why its least fold solicits each
impulsive stream until the gathered water
makes of earth a passage to the sea.

I'd like to draw a lesson from this figure,
and find some comfort in the way the larger
world rings with such dependencies.
But if I see ourselves in earth and water,
I also see one taken from the other,
the rivening wind loosed against the tree.

III

JANUARY

After days of putting down my poem
to wipe the chair, I see
the skin of the room is oozing pitch.
Steep as a church, a bishop's hat,
the roof is lined with spruce,
and this close to the stove
the heat has opened the sapline
at each dark flaw, as though it tapped
a living tree. Everyday, a pure emanation,
the syrup bleeds to the surface of the wood.

Now, a length of softwood in its craw,
the stove crackles with resin,
and the room itself
stretches and cracks with heat, cold,
the walls' mediation between them.
There are three pale coins of resin
in the usual place on the arm of the chair.
And the momentary flies,
hatched behind the wallboard
or in the pores of the old beams,
stagger down the window's white page.

If I think I am apart from this, I am a fool.
And if I think the black engine of the stove
can raise in me the same luminous waking,
I am still a fool,
since I am the one who keeps the fire.

THE APOLOGY

Hurt dogs crawl under a bush.
A hurt friend circles the house,
refusing to look in.
He makes a grave commotion in the yard
and the jay elevates the clamor of *betrayal,*
betrayal, flashing its shiny
edges from the pine.

You call through the glass.
No answer.
He's busy with his curses,
scuffing up a froth of dandelions—
isn't this what you wanted,
your own grievance, that sets the table
with one white plate?
                        Water on stones,
horses dozing upright in their stalls,
the pink of a weak sky—recalling
the tertiary theme of some great work,
you cross the grass, moving toward him
the way one greets an animal,
extending the hand.

RESCUE

But if she has eaten the food of the dead,
she cannot wholly return to the upper air.

All morning you squat in the weeds,
your head small and still
like the head of the snake at rest
on a green blade: no terror for you
in his dense body, you would follow him
into the tangle of brush by the barn
to see whatever house he keeps there.

I watch you watching the snake
or gathering the fallen bird,
the dog in the road, those stiff bodies
from whom you cannot withhold your tenderness.
As if they were your children,
they call you again and again into deep water,
as I wait on the dock,
braiding the long line that knots and tangles.

TALKING THE FIRE OUT

1.

The stanchioned cows behind him,
the assembled odors,
the dwindling closets of hay—

A farmer stands at the door of the barn:
When to plant, when to harvest:

he studies the remedial clouds,
the rehearsed fields,
red, ridged, and the air
palpable with rain.

2.

In that latitude, *come look*
might mean the long bellpull swaying
from a rafter of the barn—two snakes
mating, blacksnakes, barn snakes,
a farmer's charm;
                    might mean
bring a chair to the field and watch
a kingsnake, wrapped around a moccasin,
squeezing it like a stopped heart,
finally unwind, unhinge its jaws
and swallow the jeweled head,

the rest of it shuddering in all day
until the king sidles down the furrow
with an extra tongue.

                       Nothing is learned
by turning away. Indian summer,
when we harvested the deathweed
or cut and bound the yellow loaves of hay,
the boys brought every species
to the ninth-grade lab—king snake,
blacksnake, copperhead, cottonmouth—
and jar after jar of hazardous yield
struck at the glass.

3.

My father in the doorway
with his usual semaphore—

why is it always the same gesture
for *hello* and *goodbye?*
He keeps his elbow tucked,
like a cop,
or does he only want to ask a question?

Away from home,
I take it as a blessing,
the vertical forearm,
the seamed, outfacing palm.

4.

If you have a call,
you cradle the injured limb
and lean over the burn
as though kneeling,

but do you talk to the flesh,
to provoke its deep revulsion?
or must you sing directly
to the fire, soothing the beast
of the fire, calling it
out of the hand,
                    a poultice of words
drawing off the sultry residue
until the flush recedes,
leaving original flesh,
no blister, no scar.

5.

Who can distinguish knowledge
from belief? Against
the dangers in your own house,
you take up every weapon—

                        Listen:
my father killed a copperhead
with a switch. Out fishing,
coming on it by the pond, knowing
the exact angle and trusting it,
he flicked the weed against its back
as he had often cast his lean line
over secretive waters.

6.

Nothing is learned by turning away,
nothing surmounted.

Scattering its wise colors everywhere,
over the red barn, the red fields,
the sun is going down,
and due east, parallel on the horizon,
one of its children up-
rising catches the light
in a round bucket,

as I bend to my work, Father,
crooning over the hurt bodies,
muttering on the page.

DAUGHTER

There is one grief worse than any other.

When your small feverish throat clogged, and quit,
I knelt beside the chair on the green rug
and shook you and shook you,
but the only sound was mine shouting you back,
the delicate curls at your temples,
the blue wool blanket,
your face blue,
your jaw clamped against remedy—

how could I put a knife to that white neck?
With you in my lap,
my hands fluttering like flags,
I bend instead over your dead weight
to administer a kiss so urgent, so ruthless,
pumping breath into your stilled body,
counting out the rhythm for how long until
the second birth, the second cry
oh Jesus that sudden noisy musical inhalation
that leaves me stunned
by your survival.

LETTER FROM VERMONT

In San Francisco, spring was not a season
but an interim with rain and a gentle switch
in the wind from the sea. The bay on one side,
the clean city on the other,
we moved in the clutch of friends
down the steep steps—
                              as I pictured you
standing half in, half out of water,
you glossed the houses, history
fixed in each façade, and we received
a découpage of gardens, trees of fuchsia,
the queen's erotic earrings, and gardenias,
again in trees, the aisle among them
redolent and bruised.
                              Does it wear well,
that civil promise camouflaging rock?
The sea gives, the sea takes back,
the waves lick the women's bodies on the beach.
What is *human,* and *moral,* if not,
rising out of winter's vast denial,
this other flowering:
a deep release
such as overtakes the cloistered animals
as the last snow shreds
in the dilating pupil of the lake,
and birds return to the dull sky
their nearly legible music.

THE HAPPINESS POEMS

A small figure going up the mountain—
not really a mountain, but a cliff,
a fist of rock carved first by the river,
then by the highway, and now patched
with brush and trees. Here and there
a birch among the evergreens,
and the steady red jacket like a flag.
Surely no one could break a trail
straight up, carrying groceries—
but from here at the Amoco
someone climbs through birch and hemlock,
carrying home two large brown bags,
someone takes a shortcut
straight up the side of a mountain.

———

If there could be jubilation in the world!
The snow-draped south field
numbers four puddles of brown grass,
it's spring, there are healthy children
in the neighborhood, the lilac beginning—

———

She lost them all,
and she is someone who knows someone I know.
I try to be happy,
warming outside like a shrub,
until the siren duplicates
that cry that stops the blood.
I want to be happy
in my small unsheltered garden,
my husband a stalk in the wind's teeth,
and our two seasonal blossoms,
one Sweet William,
one delicate wood anemone.

THE BAT

Reading in bed, full of sentiment
for the mild evening and the children
asleep in adjacent rooms, hearing them
cry out now and then the brief reports
of sufficient imagination, and listening
at the same time compassionately
to the scrabble of claws, the fast treble
in the chimney—
                    then it was out,
not a trapped bird
beating at the seams of the ceiling,
but a bat lifting toward us, falling away.

Dominion over every living thing,
large brain, a choice of weapons—
Shuddering, in the lit hall
we swung repeatedly against
its rising secular face
until it fell; then
shoveled it into the yard for the cat
who shuttles easily between two worlds.

SWEET EVERLASTING

Swarming over the damp ground with pocket lenses
that discover and distort like an insect's
compound eye, the second grade
slows, stops at the barrier on the path.
They straddle the horizontal trunk, down for months;
rub the rough track of the saw, then focus
on the new shoots at the other end—
residual, suggestive.
I follow the children into open land
above the orchard, its small clouds tethered
to the grass, where we gather
samples of the plentiful white bud
that stipples the high pasture, and name it
by the book: wooly stem, pale lanceolate leaves;
the one called Everlasting. The punishment for doubt
is doubt—my father's death has taught me that.
Last week, he surfaced in a dream as promised,
as, at night, the logic of earth subsides
and stars appear to substantiate
what we could not see. But when I woke,
I remembered nothing that could tell me
which among those distant pulsing inconclusive signs
were active, which extinguished—
remembered, that is,
nothing that could save him.

FOR MY MOTHER

When does the soul leave the body?
Since early morning you have not moved—
only your head moves, thrown back
with each deliberate breath,
the one sound that matters in the room.
My brother is here, my sister,
two of your sisters, ripples
widening from the bed.
The nurses check and measure,
keeping the many records.
Are you afraid?
Are you dreaming of what is past, lost,
or is this sleep some other preparation?
My sister has put your rings
on my finger; it seems like your hand
stroking the white brow,
unable to release you,
not even after you have asked for death—

And we know nothing about such pain,
except that it has weaned you from us,
and from the reedy, rusted
sunflowers outside the window,
drooping over the snow like tongueless bells.

FOR MY FATHER

1. Elegy

Turning from a loss,
as if turning from an open window,
its local composition:
limbs juxtaposed against the sky,
juncture of sky and hillock,
the stark debrided tree.

Autumn, and the shucked leaves
are eating *green,* absorbing it
even as they are severed or detaching—
red is what red leaves repel. Any abstraction
names a consequence.

He is not here
He is not here

Halfway through a life, seeing leaves
the color of fire and of wounds
swaddle the base of the broad
deciduous tree,
you turn from the window's

slice of terrible radiance
to face the cluttered interior on which it falls.

2. Pittsylvania County

In the front yard, my father and his son
are playing ball, the round egg arcs
toward a lap of brown leather, the sound
of an axe on green wood, a bass
hitting the water. The boy
could do this forever—only one glove
between them and he has it—the fireflies
already discernible on the hillside,
the grass wet, he doesn't falter
as he skirts the waist-high crabapple
or backs across the graveled drive.
What am I after? Not shagging flies
on the lawn with my father, and not
drying the last dish with a fresh towel.
My father is a stationary target
through increasing dark, and out from my brother's
cocked proficient arm, the ball leaps,
of its own volition, into his hand.

3. New England Graveyard

It is a foreign symmetry, unlike anything
in the earth's surface rubble—
the headstones, grouped by family
to organize the sacred rows; the flowers
at the fresh site
are forced blooms with exposed
glands of pollen and the widest throats;
even the neat packages
of food, each container marked
with the names of the living.
If there is a life beyond the body,
I think we have no use for order
but are buoyed past our individuating fear,
and that memory is not,
as now, a footprint filling with water.